For Eleanor, who wanted a book with
Santa on every page.

And with special thanks to Aaron Sharff
for his extensive editorial assistance.

—B.S.

This book is for my jolly husband, Dax Santa.
I mean Santi! I love you more than
Christmas cookies.

—E.K.

DIAL BOOKS FOR YOUNG READERS • An imprint of Penguin Random House LLC, New York

First published in the United States of America by Dial Books for Young Readers, an imprint of Penguin Random House LLC, 2022

Text copyright © 2022 by Billy Sharff
Illustrations copyright © 2022 by Eda Kaban

Dial & colophon are registered trademarks of Penguin Random House LLC.

Visit us online at penguinrandomhouse.com.

Library of Congress Cataloging-in-Publication Data is available.

Printed in the USA | ISBN 9780593325230

1 3 5 7 9 10 8 6 4 2
PC
Design by Jason Henry | Text set in Archer

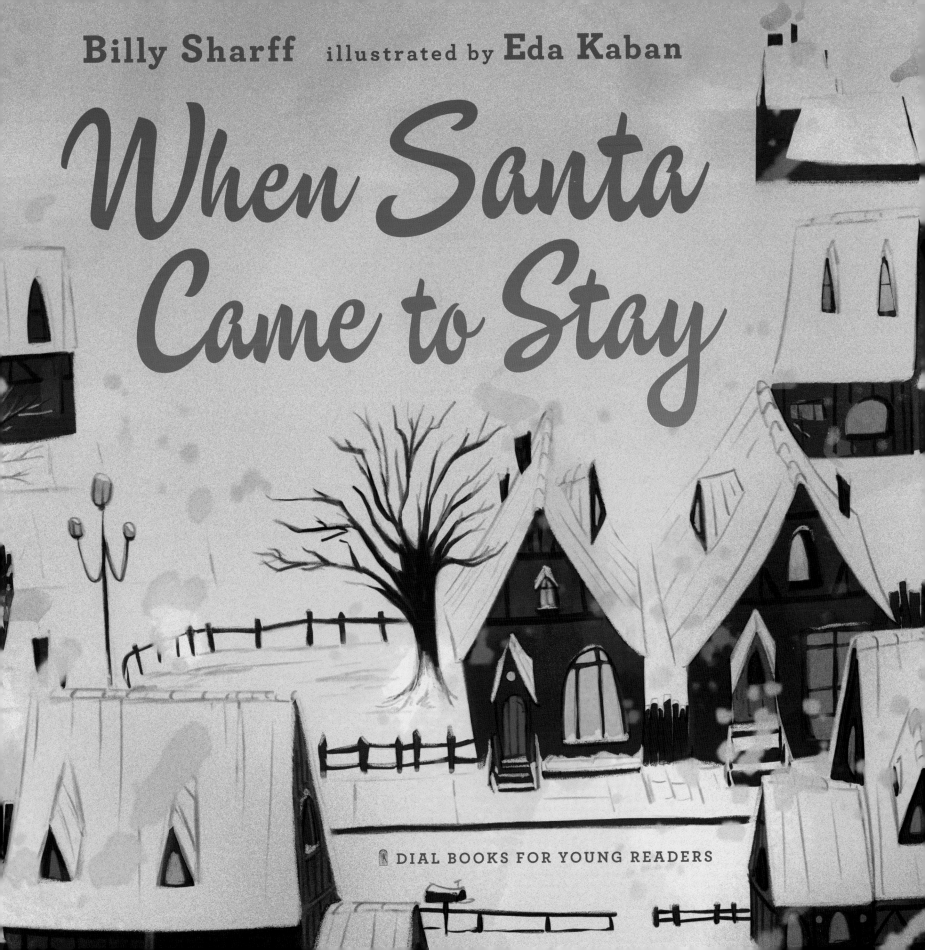

Billy Sharff   illustrated by Eda Kaban

When Santa Came to Stay

DIAL BOOKS FOR YOUNG READERS

When Santa Claus came by last year,
He liked our cookies so...

He came again on New Year's Eve
And did not want to go.

His Missus came on Valentine's.
(She missed her Mr. Claus.)

She brought along their baby.
And their kitten, Santa Paws.

On Easter came the in-laws.
And both of them got stuck.

They brought along the Easter Bunny,
And her babies Chuck—
And Puck and Buck and Tuck and Zuck
And Huck and Luck and Duck.

On Mother's Day
came Santa's mom.

On Father's Day?
You get it.

We welcomed one and all to stay.
(We thought we might regret it.)

At first it sure was fun to call
Each morning Christmas morning.

Every time I turned,
I got a present
without warning.

The toys went on for miles!
The yo-yos, trains, and kites!

The songs!
The laughs!

The bubble baths!

The midnight reindeer flights!

Each meal was full of Christmas cheer,
With treats and sweets to spare—
With eggnog in our cereal,
Confetti in our hair!

So we were pretty sick of them
By Independence Day.

"I've had it up to HERE!" said Dad.
"These Clauses cannot stay!"

We slipped them carrot cookies.
We thought they'd really hate 'em.
But when the reindeer caught a whiff,
They piled in and ate 'em!

And so we LOCKED THEM OUT!
We even LOCKED THE FLUE!

But they came through the dryer vent.
(I'm more surprised than you!)
"We've gotten sick of Christmas!" I said to ol' Saint Nick.
"But this is so much fun!" said Santa. "Do you want a lick?"

Mama called up Mayor Jane. But then . . .
She just joined in.
"I'm staying off the naughty list!"
she giggled, with a grin.

We had to think of something.
We had to get them OUT,

Or they would stay
the *whole year through*,
I hadn't any doubt.

And so I hatched a cunning plan. "Come on!" I said. "Let's bake!"
We baked the *sweetest* cookies that it's possible to make!

"Hurray!" they cheered and asked for more. "These cookies are a dream!"
And then they slurped up eggnog, which was made with heavy cream.

Next, I gave out gifts—they ripped and shredded them with glee.
Every time they opened one, I gave another three.

But there was just ONE race car.
I told them they could share.

"Santa's hogging it!" they wailed.
"Come on! This isn't fair!"

"My turn's not done!" cried Santa Claus, which started quite a fight.
I couldn't help but gawk. Oh, what a strange, unpleasant sight!

Then Santa skidded on a cake
And fell into the tree.

Down he came—
with an EEEK!
AAK!

THUMP!—landing right on me.

I heaved ol' Santa off the floor. He helped to wipe me clean.
And then he rubbed his eyes, like he was waking from a dream.

I said:
"Oh, Santa, can't you see that none of this is right?
Look around you—

This is not what Christmas should be like.

"Christmas isn't all about the presents and the sweets.
It's so much more than glitter, ribbons, shiny toys, and treats.

"Christmas is for family. And singing in the park.

"Christmas is for hanging lights, when all the world is dark.

"Christmas is for helping out, when someone needs a friend.

"And even though it's very sad . . .

"Christmas has to end."

"Of course you're right,"
sighed Santa Claus.
"*That's* the Christmas Way!
I can't believe we stayed so long
And went so far astray."

They cleaned the house, and said goodbye.
And then they hit the sky.

How nice it was to be alone,
just Mama, Dad, and I.

After that, I went back to my normal, simple life.
And when next Christmas Eve arrived, it really *did* feel nice—
The sights, the smells, the silver bells. My heart was full of cheer!

But we made VERY sure they wouldn't stay again this year.